RICHARD SCARRY'S
Great Big Schoolhouse
Readers

Go, Huckle, Go!

Illustrated by Huck Scarry
Written by Erica Farber

STERLING CHILDREN'S BOOKS
New York

Today is race day.

Hooray!

Time to get ready.

Huckle and Lowly get

Huckle's truck.

Huckle washes his truck.

Lowly washes the truck, too.

Huckle checks the tires.

He blows them up.

Huckle checks the brakes.

"Look out, Huckle!"

All set.

Huckle and Lowly

go to the race.

The cars and trucks get set to go.

One, two, three—go!
Zoom! Zoom!

The cars and trucks race.

Skip is first.

Skip is fast.

Oh, no!

Go, Huckle, go!

See Bridget go.

Bridget's tire pops.

Go, Huckle, go!

See Frances go.

Poof! Look at all the smoke!

Go, Huckle, go!

See Ella go.

See the mud.

Ella's car is stuck. Yuck!

Go, Huckle, go!

See Arthur go.

There goes his stuff!

Oh, no!

Molly's wheels fall off.

Look out!

Stop those wheels.

Go, Huckle, go!

Huckle wins the race!
Hooray for Huckle!

STERLING CHILDREN'S BOOKS
New York

An Imprint of Sterling Publishing
387 Park Avenue South
New York, NY 10016

ISBN 978-1-4549-1307-8

Produced by

 JR Sansevere

Distributed in Canada by Sterling Publishing
C/o Canadian Manda Group, 165 Dufferin Street
Toronto, Ontario, Canada M6K 3H6
Distributed in the United Kingdom by GMC Distribution Services
Castle Place, 166 High Street, Lewes, East Sussex, England BN7 1XU
Distributed in Australia by Capricorn Link (Australia) Pty. Ltd.
P.O. Box 704, Windsor, NSW 2756, Australia

For information about custom editions, special sales, premium and corporate purchases,
please contact Sterling Special Sales at 800-805-5489 or specialsales@sterlingpublishing.com.

Printed in China

Lot #:
2 4 6 8 10 9 7 5 3 1
12/13

www.sterlingpublishing.com/kids

RICHARD SCARRY'S
Great Big Schoolhouse
Readers

One of the best-selling children's author/illustrators of all time, Richard Scarry has taught generations of children about the world around them—from the alphabet to counting, identifying colors, and even exploring a day at school.

Though Scarry's books are educational, they are beloved for their charming characters, wacky sense of humor, and frenetic energy. Scarry considered himself an entertainer first, and an educator second. He once said, "Everything has an educational value if you look for it. But it's the FUN I want to get across."

A prolific artist, Richard Scarry created more than 300 books, and they have sold over 200 million copies worldwide and have been translated into 30 languages. Richard Scarry died in 1994, but his incredible legacy continues with new books illustrated by his son, Huck Scarry.